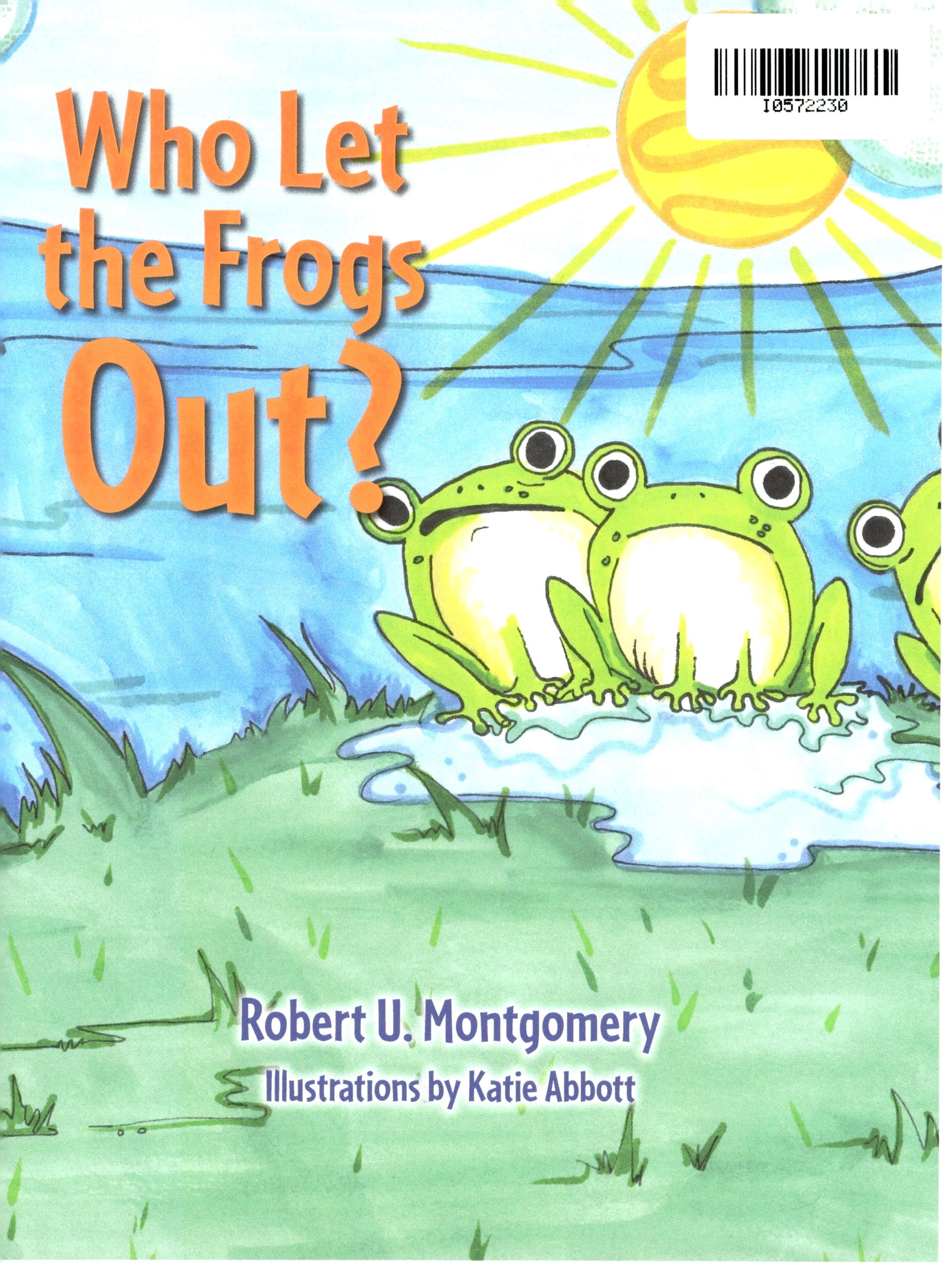

Who Let
the Frogs
Out?
Robert U. Montgomery
Illustrations by Katie Abbott

Who Let the Frogs Out?
Robert U. Montgomery
RUM Publishing

Published by RUM Publishing, Bonne Terre, MO

Illustrations: Katie Abbott

Cover and Interior design: Davis Creative, www.DavisCreative.com

Library of Congress Cataloging-in-Publication Data

Library of Congress Control Number: 2019905878

Robert U. Montgomery

Who Let the Frogs Out?

ISBN: 978-1-7330033-2-2

Library of Congress subject headings:

1. JUV001000 JUVENILE FICTION / Action & Adventure / General   2. JUV019000 JUVENILE FICTION / Humorous Stories   3. JUV002000 JUVENILE FICTION / Animals / General

2019

    During summer, my friends and I always had plenty to keep us busy. We rode our bikes and played baseball. We went fishing down at the creek. We once almost caught something besides a fish too! Droopy, Carl's Basset Hound, really wanted a taste of the raw bacon that we used to catch catfish. But he was too fat to jump high enough to grab Benny's baited hook when he made a cast. After that, we left Droopy at home.

    Also we had turtle races. It took us awhile to figure out that the only way we could have a turtle race is to put them in the center of a circle. They just wouldn't go in a straight line, no matter how hard we tried to steer them! We also learned that turtles love strawberries!

In the evenings, we'd play lots of games that included running and/or hiding. One of my favorites was "Red Light, Green Light, Stop!" Everybody but the person who was "it" lined up at the starting line and faced the finish line. The "it" person stood at the finish line, with his back turned to the others.

When he said, "green light," we'd start running toward the finish line. But at any moment, he could say "red light" and whirl around to face us. Anyone caught moving after he said "red light" had to go back to the start. The person who made it to the finish first was winner and the last became "it." Key to winning was to run, but not so fast that you couldn't stop quickly. Sometimes, I'd just throw myself on the ground to keep from getting caught. I tore the knees out of my jeans that way, and Mom wasn't too happy about that.

When it got dark enough, we'd chase and catch fireflies, which our parents also called "lightning bugs." One night, Matt said that we should feed some of the bugs to a toad. "I'll bet his belly would light up," he said.

And he was right. It did! A little ball of light bounced up and down on the road in the dark as the toad hopped away. We laughed until our sides hurt. And the toad got a free supper, so I think that he liked it too.

Matt was like the "mad scientist" of our group that we called "The Four Musketeers." He made the best grades and knew lots of stuff that the rest of us didn't. My name is Bobby. And I tell you all about our gang – Matt, Carl, Benny, and me – in *Who Let the Bugs Out?* If you haven't read it, you should!

But no matter how much fun we had playing and exploring in and around our neighborhood, what we looked forward to the most during summer was spending two days at my grandparents' house in the country.

PapPa had a pond and we could catch really big catfish there. He taught us how to clean them, too, and then MamMa fried them up for us. We thought that there was nothing better than eating fish that we had just caught

ourselves! She served them with cole slaw, baked beans, and hush puppies, followed by homemade apple pie and ice cream. She didn't even mind when Carl asked for more pie and ice cream. – a third time!

PapPa said that cornbread fried in little balls was called "hush puppies" because that's what men used to say when they tossed the treats to their hunting dogs. As the men sat around a campfire having supper, the dogs howled and they wanted them to shut up. MamMa said he was making that up.

PapPa let us help feed the cows and chickens too, although we had to get up early to do that. Of course, that wasn't a problem, since a rooster liked to crow at sunrise right outside our windows. The cows were stinky, if you want to know the truth. And not stinky in a good way, like when you pass gas and make your little sister gag and say "Oh, gross!"

No, they were stinky because of all the cow pies that they left in the pasture, just waiting for someone to step in. At one time or another, we all stepped in one – or two or three. That's why MamMa had us take off our shoes on the back porch.

Even more than Mom, she seemed to spend a lot of time cleaning her house, especially pushing a vacuum cleaner all over the place.

Once I mentioned that to Mom and she laughed. "Maybe that's because she has four 11-year-old boys staying there," she said. "One is more than enough for me."

Also, MamMa and PapPa shared their house with Ol' Fred, a goofy yellow Lab, and Ol' Marge, a gray and white cat, who delighted in tormenting Ol' Fred. When the dog finally ran out of patience, he chased Ol' Marge under a bed or up onto the top of the refrigerator, or "ice box," as MamMa called it. Their hair was another reason that MamMa vacuumed so much.

The four of us shared a room in the back of the house. It had two big beds that were the best in the world for bouncing on. PapPa called them "feather beds." The mattresses were filled with goose feathers, which is what made them so soft and springy.

The bed frames were high off the floor, too, so sometimes it almost felt like I was going to bump my head on the ceiling. With all that pie and ice cream in him, Carl wasn't in much danger of doing that.

Every summer trip to my grandparents with the Four Musketeers was so much fun that it would be difficult to say that one was better than the other. But one definitely was the most memorable, because of something that happened on the morning that Dad was to pick us up and take us back home. In fact, I'd say that it's just as memorable as that night we smuggled a jar full of fireflies into my bedroom at home and someone turned them loose while the rest of us were asleep.

If you asked my grandparents, I'm sure that they'd agree, especially MamMa. Even before the rooster crowed to wake us up, we heard her screaming. And when we ran to the kitchen, we saw her dancing on the table, yelling "Ernest! Ernest! Help me! Do something!"

That's was how I found out PapPa's real name. But that wasn't what made that day so memorable.

That started the afternoon before. We were fishing at the pond when suddenly Carl yelled, "Hey, guys, look at that!"

Just down the bank from us, we saw little frogs crawling up out of the water. Based on their size, they probably were cricket frogs, Matt said.

In school, we had learned that frogs are amphibians, which means they live part of their lives in the water and part on land. They lay their eggs in water and the babies start out as tadpoles with gills. As they grow, tadpoles develop legs and lungs, while they lose their fishlike tails.

Salamanders are amphibians too, and we had seen some of those at the pond also. They were black with yellow spots.

With our rods anchored to keep fish from pulling them in, we ran down to get a closer look at the frogs. On our first trip to the pond, we quickly had learned how a catfish will take your rod if you're not holding it or have it secured with a wire holder. One of them stole Carl's rod when he sat it down to get another soda out of the cooler.

After staring in disbelief at the place in the water where the rod disappeared, Benny and I waded in to try to find it. Finally, he felt it with his foot, picked it up, and reeled in a nice catfish.

"That's my rod. That's my fish!" Carl said. We booed and Benny splashed water on him.

"In your dreams," he said and splattered Carl some more.

Carl waded in and splashed back. And that's how we ended up taking off all our clothes on the back porch, in addition to our shoes.

But we wouldn't have to get wet to catch the frogs. They were right there on the bank. Matt said, "Looks like they aren't tadpoles anymore. No tails or anything."

"We should catch some and take them home," Benny said. "We have an empty aquarium in our basement. We can make a home for them in that."

"But what will we feed them?" Carl asked.

"What do you think *cricket* frogs eat?" I asked, and we all laughed.

Really, I had read in a science book that cricket frogs in the wild eat mostly mosquitoes, not crickets. They got their name because they sound like crickets. But I was pretty certain that they would eat crickets, just like turtles eat strawberries, even though they don't buy them in a store.

We always brought a little plastic terrarium with us when we came to visit–just in case. We had used it often too, taking home fence lizards, ring-necked snakes, and once even a field mouse. "You are *not* bringing that rodent in this house," Mom had said.

After Benny ran back to the house to get the terrarium, we started filling it with baby cricket frogs. Compared to bull frogs, they were pretty easy to catch. But by the time that we had what looked like a couple of dozen in the terrarium, we were hot, sweaty, and ready to go back to the house. After we showered, we knew that MamMa would have lemonade and chocolate chip cookies waiting for us.

And that's what we did. As always, we took off our shoes on the porch. "What about the frogs?" Carl asked. "Should we leave them out here?"

"No," Matt said. "Looks like a thunderstorm is coming. Wind might turn it over or it might fill up with rain."

So we shoved the terrarium under a feather bed and forgot about it—until early the next morning when we heard MamMa screaming. As she danced on the kitchen table, she held her bathrobe up around her knees, as if that would help protect her from the frogs all over the floor.

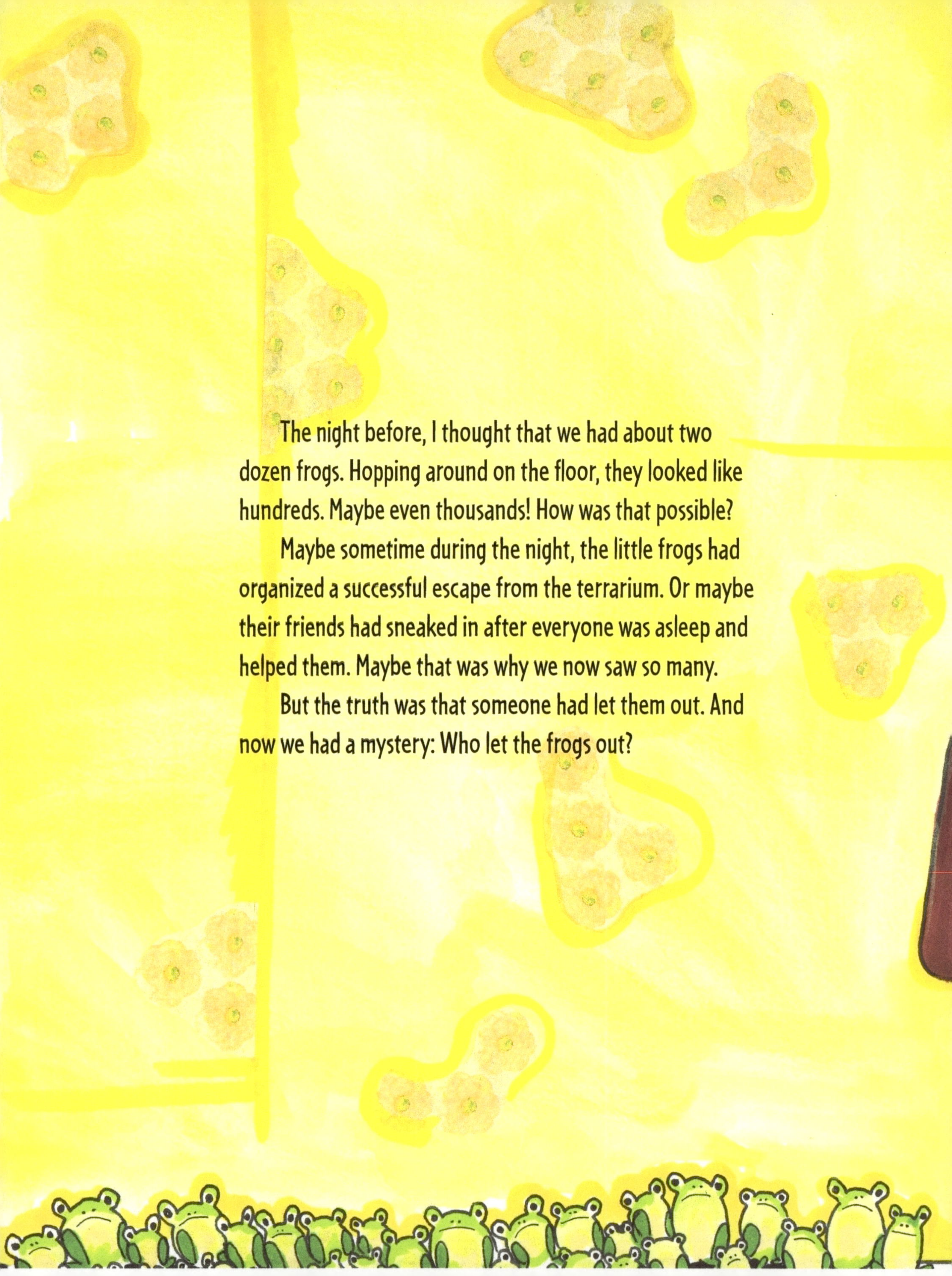

The night before, I thought that we had about two dozen frogs. Hopping around on the floor, they looked like hundreds. Maybe even thousands! How was that possible?

Maybe sometime during the night, the little frogs had organized a successful escape from the terrarium. Or maybe their friends had sneaked in after everyone was asleep and helped them. Maybe that was why we now saw so many.

But the truth was that someone had let them out. And now we had a mystery: Who let the frogs out?

Before solving the mystery, though, we had to help PapPa catch the frogs and put them back in the terrarium. Ol' Fred wasn't any help. He came in to check out the craziness, yawned, and went back to bed. Ol' Marge wanted to help, but PapPa locked her in the bathroom. MamMa stopped dancing and pointed out frogs that she feared might get away.

"Get that one over by the trash can," she said. "And get that one before it goes into the living room!"

Finally, we captured the escapees--- most of them anyway--- and suddenly they looked like only a couple of dozen again. Matt and I watched two of them hop under the refrigerator but thought it best not to mention it. We made certain the terrarium lid was on tight, and set it out on the porch.

"Are you sure you got them all?" MamMa asked, as she climbed off the table and headed to the bathroom. PapPa assured her that we had and started cooking breakfast.

He wasn't nearly as good a cook as MamMa. As we ate his dry scrambled eggs, burnt toast, and extra crispy bacon, he put his fork down and looked at all of us.

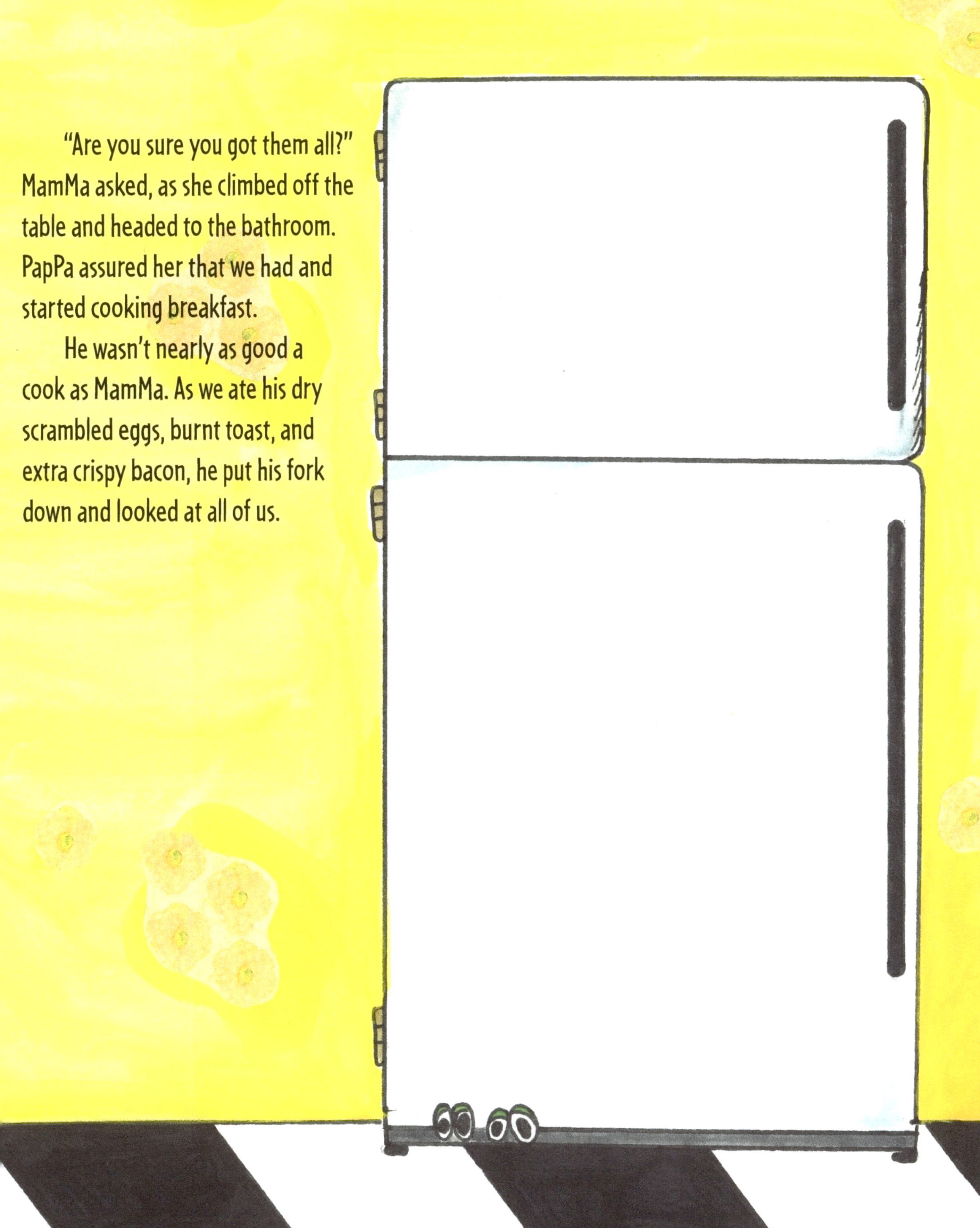

"Someone turned those frogs loose," he said. "I'm really disappointed in someone here. I won't embarrass you by trying to find out who.

"But turning those frogs loose was a very childish thing to do, and I expected better from my grandson and his friends."

By not asking one of us to confess, PapPa made us all feel guilty. I glanced around at my three friends, each one shook his head, telling me that he didn't do it. And I knew that I didn't.

"PapPa, none of us did it. We know it was a bad idea to bring the frogs inside and put them under the bed," I said. "But none of us did it. I promise."

Carl nodded his head in agreement. He often the gets blame for practical jokes, like putting worms in Matt's jean pockets while we were having a sleepover. And he usually gets the blame because he's guilty.

But not this time. I was sure of it. "Maybe the dog or cat did it," he said. "Maybe Ol' Fred chased Ol' Marge under the bed and she knocked over the terrarium."

PapPa rubbed his stubbly chin. "I guess that's possible," he said. "But after you boys came in last night, I didn't see them running around. Did you?"

We shook our heads. "You're right," I said. "And if they had done it after we went to bed, we would have heard them."

We played with our food instead of eating it, more because we were embarrassed than because it didn't taste good, which it didn't.

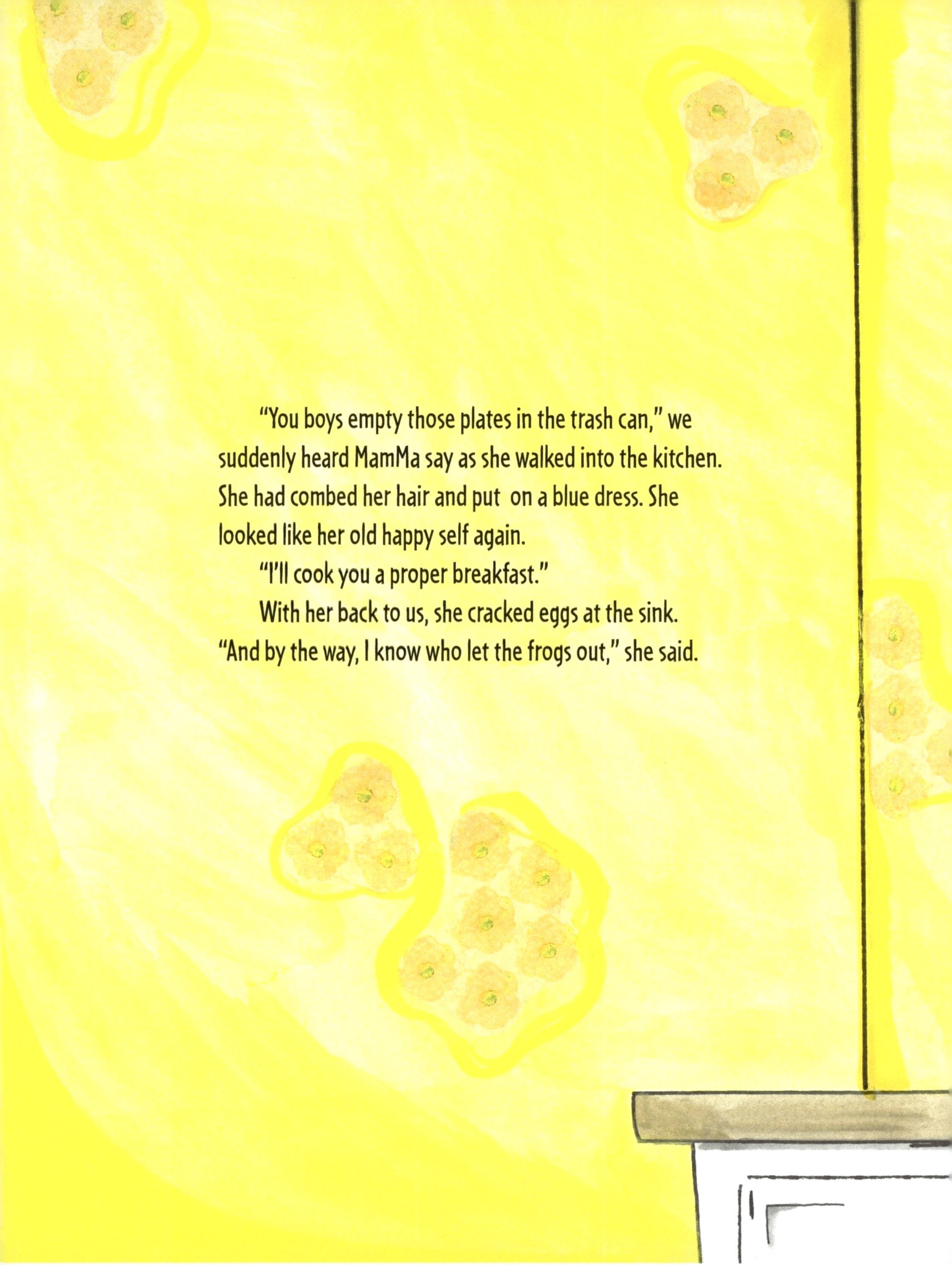

"You boys empty those plates in the trash can," we
suddenly heard MamMa say as she walked into the kitchen.
She had combed her hair and put on a blue dress. She
looked like her old happy self again.

"I'll cook you a proper breakfast."

With her back to us, she cracked eggs at the sink.
"And by the way, I know who let the frogs out," she said.

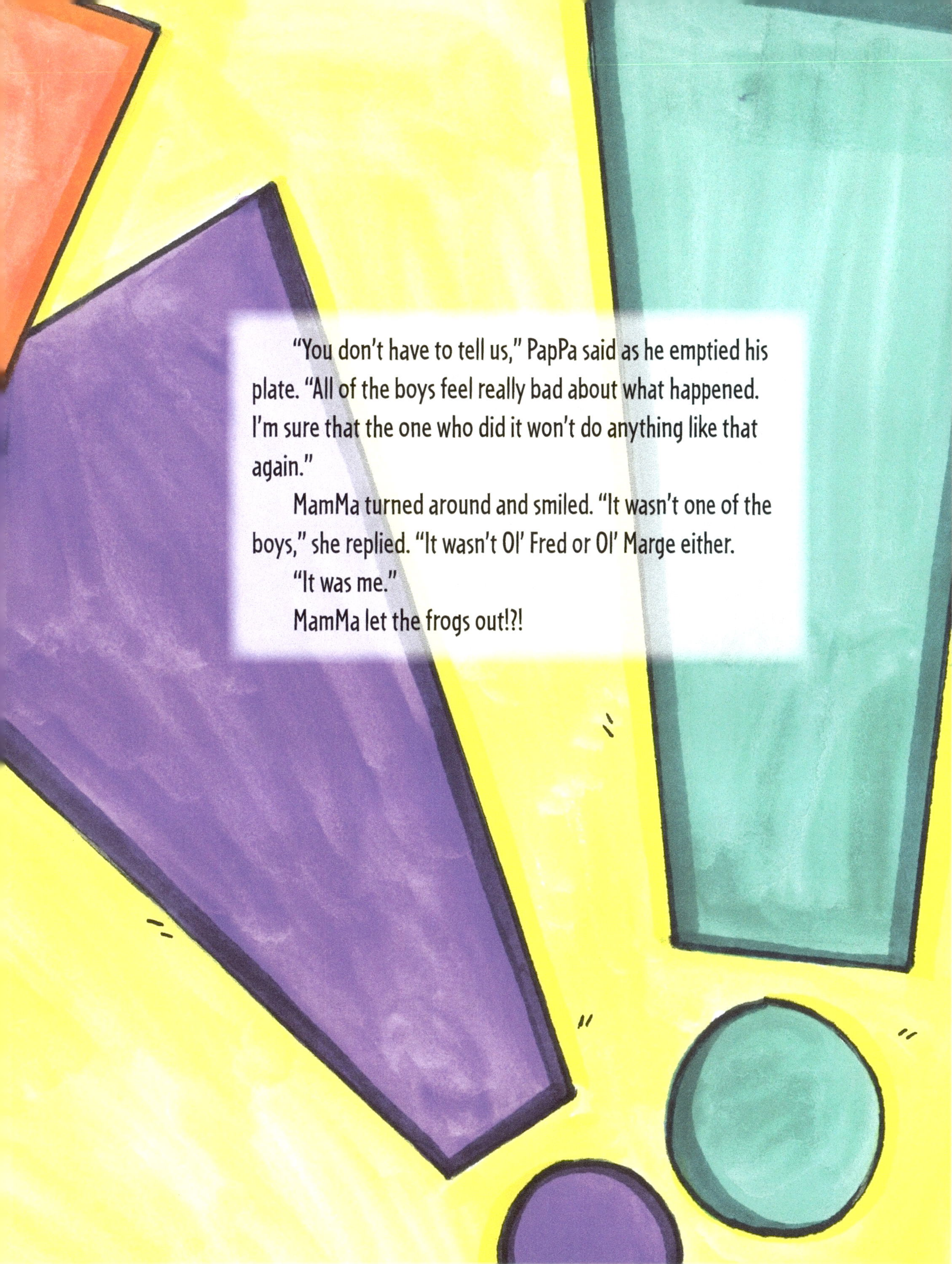

"You don't have to tell us," PapPa said as he emptied his plate. "All of the boys feel really bad about what happened. I'm sure that the one who did it won't do anything like that again."

MamMa turned around and smiled. "It wasn't one of the boys," she replied. "It wasn't Ol' Fred or Ol' Marge either.

"It was me."
MamMa let the frogs out!?!

"While you boys watched TV with Ernest, I vacuumed your room," she said. "I ran the vacuum under your beds, like I always do. I must have turned over the terrarium and didn't realize it. That must have knocked off the top."

She smiled at us again, a sweet grandmother smile. "But boys, please don't bring any more critters in the house. Okay?"

We quickly promised that we would not.

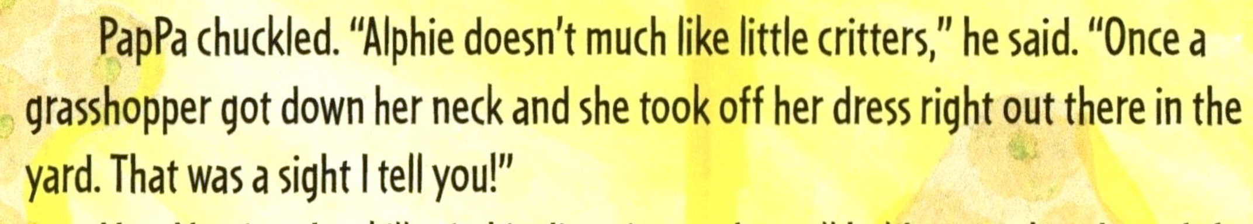

PapPa chuckled. "Alphie doesn't much like little critters," he said. "Once a grasshopper got down her neck and she took off her dress right out there in the yard. That was a sight I tell you!"

MamMa aimed a skillet in his direction and we all held up our hands to defend ourselves.

But she didn't throw it.

"Fortunately, it was a warm day," she said, and then smiled.

Years later, as an adult, I still fondly remember that day when my grandmother could have left us all feeling bad and didn't. She took responsibility for her actions, instead of letting others unfairly take the blame.

And she laughed at herself as well, which reminded us all never to take ourselves too seriously.

About the Author

Author Robert U. Montgomery loves nature and teaching. Those passions are reflected in most of his works, including *Who Let the Bugs Out?*, an illustrated children's book, and *Fish, Frogs, and Fireflies: Growing up with Nature*. Additional titles include *Pippa's Journey: Tail-Wagging Tales of Rescue Dogs*, and *Under the Bed: Tales From an Innocent Childhood*. The award-winning author's short stories and nature photos have been published in both adult and children's publications, including *Boy's Life*. He also has written three books about fishing and an eco-thriller novel, *Revenge of the Wolf*. Montgomery lives in the Missouri Ozarks with his rescue dog Pippa.

RUM Publishing.com